Dear Parents:

Congratulations! Your child is taking the first steps on an exciting journey. The destination? Independent reading!

STEP INTO READING® will help your child get there. The program offers five steps to reading success. Each step includes fun stories and colorful art or photographs. In addition to original fiction and books with favorite characters, there are Step into Reading Non-Fiction Readers, Phonics Readers and Boxed Sets, Sticker Readers, and Comic Readers—a complete literacy program with something to interest every child.

Learning to Read, Step by Step!

Ready to Read   Preschool–Kindergarten
• big type and easy words • rhyme and rhythm • picture clues
For children who know the alphabet and are eager to begin reading.

Reading with Help   Preschool–Grade 1
• basic vocabulary • short sentences • simple stories
For children who recognize familiar words and sound out new words with help.

Reading on Your Own   Grades 1–3
• engaging characters • easy-to-follow plots • popular topics
For children who are ready to read on their own.

Reading Paragraphs   Grades 2–3
• challenging vocabulary • short paragraphs • exciting stories
For newly independent readers who read simple sentences with confidence.

Ready for Chapters   Grades 2–4
• chapters • longer paragraphs • full-color art
For children who want to take the plunge into chapter books but still like colorful pictures.

STEP INTO READING® is designed to give every child a successful reading experience. The grade levels are only guides; children will progress through the steps at their own speed, developing confidence in their reading. The F&P Text Level on the back cover serves as another tool to help you choose the right book for your child.

Remember, a lifetime love of reading starts with a single step!

To Mary, my best friend
—M.C.

Text copyright © 2017 by Margery Cuyler
Cover art and interior illustrations copyright © 2017 by David L. Walker

Visit us on the Web!
StepIntoReading.com
randomhousekids.com

Educators and librarians, for a variety of teaching tools,
visit us at RHTeachersLibrarians.com

Library of Congress Cataloging-in-Publication Data
Names: Cuyler, Margery, author. | Walker, David L., illustrator.
Title: Best friends / Margery Cuyler, David L. Walker.
Description: New York : Random House, [2017] | Series: Step into reading. Step 1 |
Summary: When his best friend Sue finds a new friend at school,
Pete feels dejected until Sue invites everyone to play together.
Identifiers: LCCN 2015043657 (print) | LCCN 2016020401 (ebook) |
ISBN 978-0-399-55369-1 (trade pbk.) | ISBN 978-0-399-55370-7 (lib. bdg.) |
ISBN 978-0-399-55371-4 (ebook)
Subjects: | CYAC: Stories in rhyme. | Best friends—Fiction. | Friendship—Fiction.
Classification: LCC PZ8.3.C99 Be 2017 (print) | LCC PZ8.3.C99 (ebook) |
DDC [E]—dc23

Printed in the United States of America
10 9 8 7 6 5 4 3 2 1

This book has been officially leveled by using the F&P Text Level Gradient™ Leveling System.

Best Friends

by Margery Cuyler
illustrated by David L. Walker

Random House 🏠 New York

My best friend
is Pete.

Pete lives
on my street.

Pete and I play.

We play every day.

We play with my pup.

8

We like to dress up.

Pete is a knight.

I am Snow White.

I meet someone new.

Her name is Sue.

Sue goes to my school.

I think she is cool.

She and I play.

Pete stays away.

18

He plays by himself
near the toy shelf.

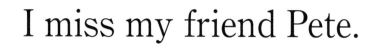

I miss my friend Pete.

Hey!
My two friends
can meet!

22

I invite them today
to come over
and play.

We play with my pup.

Then we all dress up.

Pete is a cat.

I wear a hat.

26

Sue wears a gown
and a pink crown.

Together we play.

We have a great day.

I love *both* my friends.

They are the best.